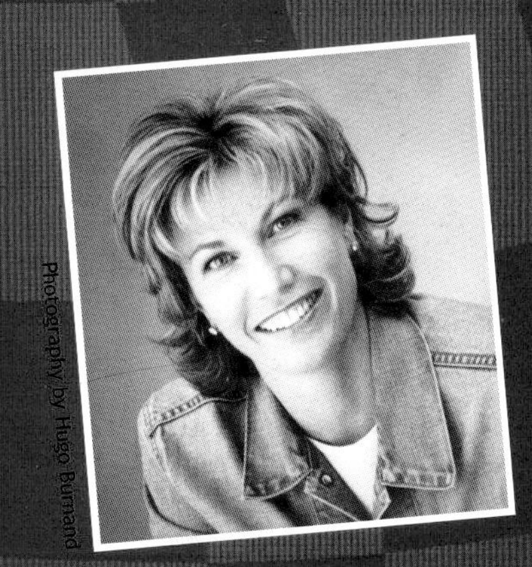
Photography by Hugo Burnand

THE AUTHOR

Lisa Dennis is the wife of Ron, Team Principal of the McLaren Formula One Team. She loves travelling the world, attending all the races. Her many amazing experiences — and her own inventive children — have inspired her to create Mac & Lauren.

POCKET BOOKS
An imprint of Simon & Schuster UK Ltd. Africa House, 64-78 Kingsway, London WC2B 6AH
A Viacom Company
First published in Great Britain by Simon & Schuster UK Ltd, 2003

A CIP catalogue record for this book is available from the British Library
ISBN 0 743 46784 1
1 3 5 7 9 10 8 6 4 2

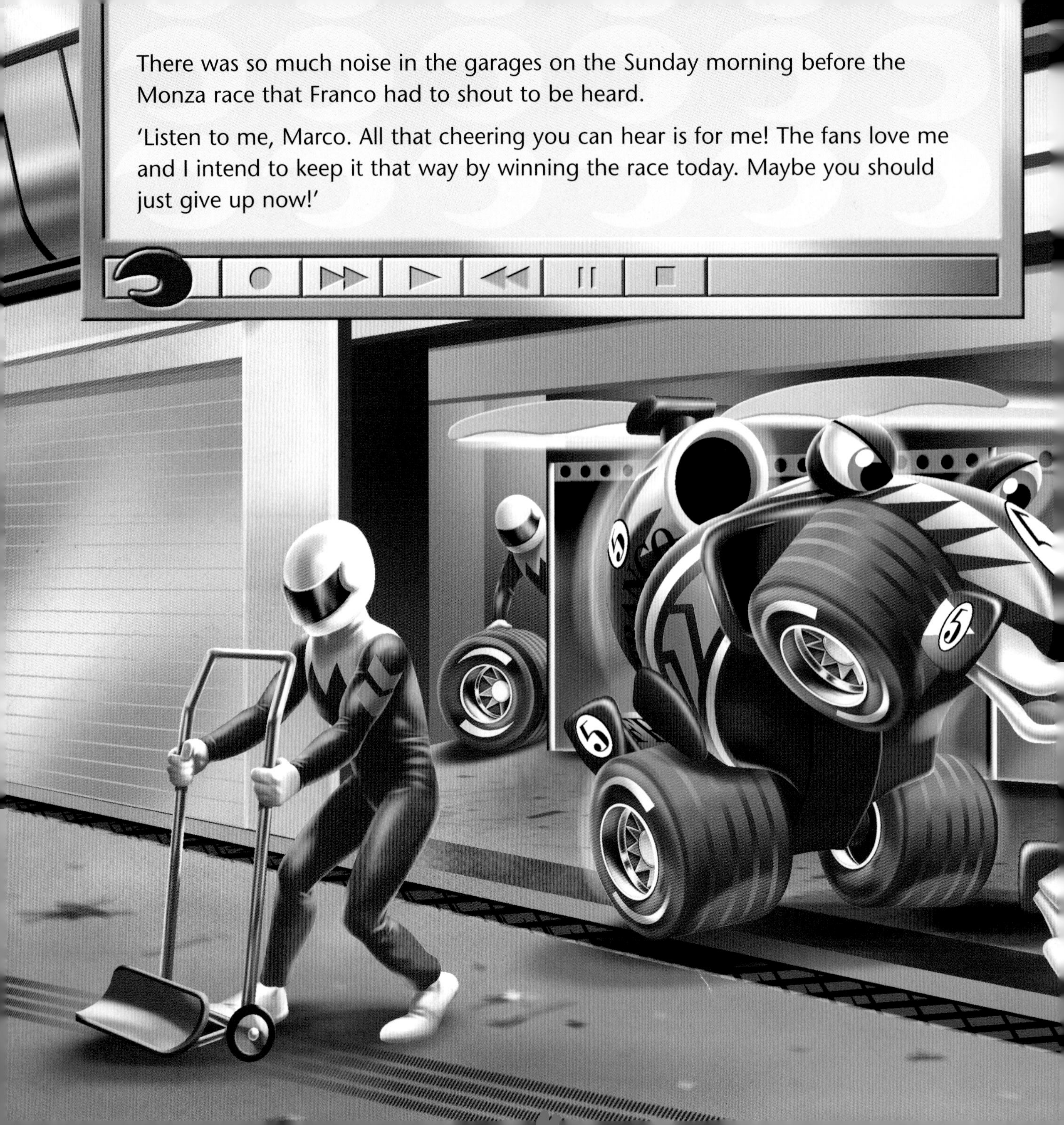

There was so much noise in the garages on the Sunday morning before the Monza race that Franco had to shout to be heard.

'Listen to me, Marco. All that cheering you can hear is for me! The fans love me and I intend to keep it that way by winning the race today. Maybe you should just give up now!'

Franco roared so loudly that Lauren overheard him in the next garage.

'That Franco is big-headed and so mean to his team-mate. I feel sorry for Marco. Gosh, I'm glad we don't treat each other like that, Mac,' she said.

'I like having you as a team-mate, Lauren, and, besides, if we stick together and help each other, we have a better chance of winning,' replied Mac.

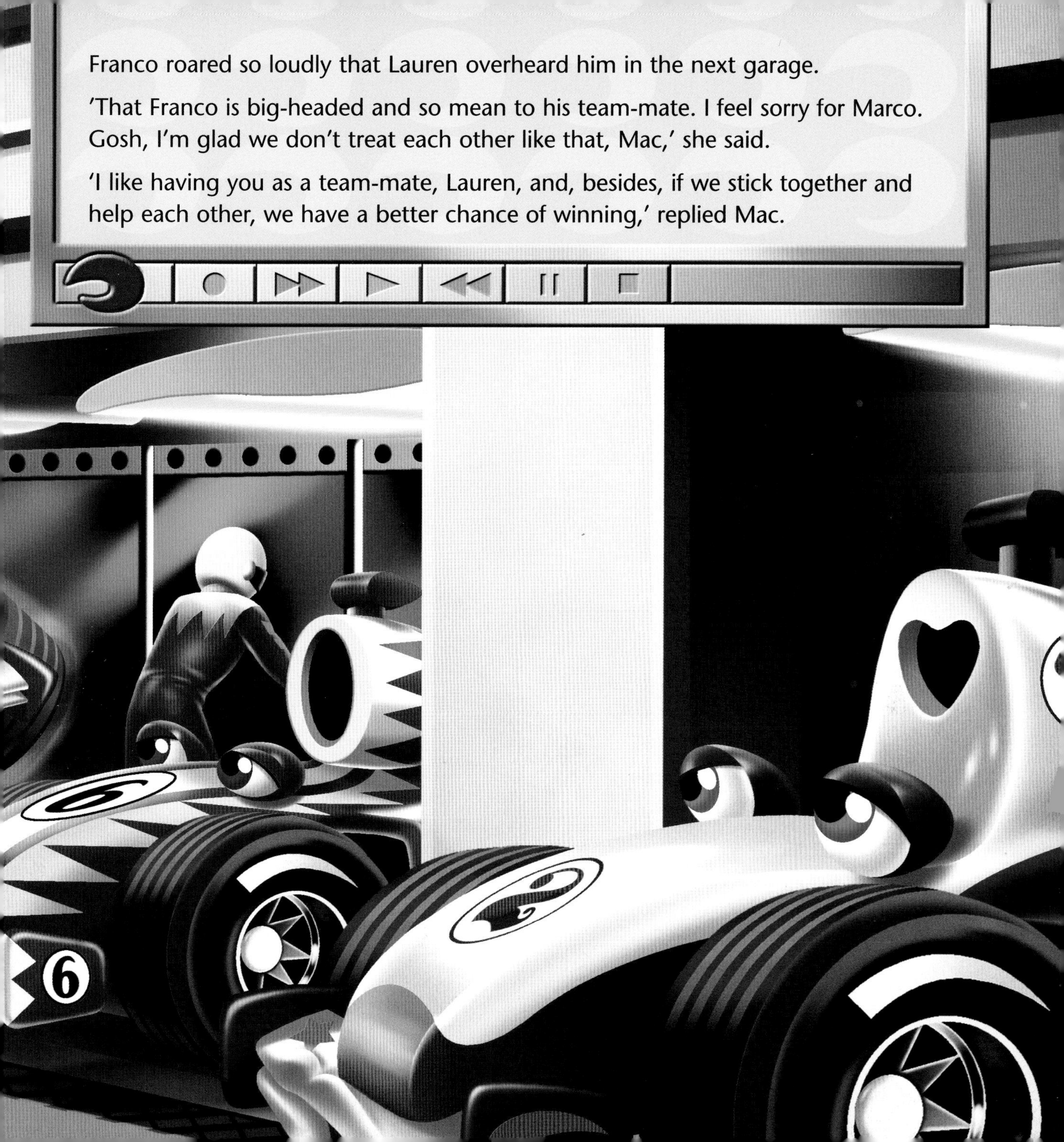

7
5

Before the race, all of the cars were called to a safety meeting with Race Control.

‘The first corner is very dangerous. Do you all agree not to overtake until all the cars are safely through?” boomed Race Control.

‘I don’t agree! I’m here to race whether it’s safe or not. That is what my adoring public came to see,’ bragged Franco.

‘You mean they didn’t come to see you start in fifth place because you qualified so badly?’ Bruno taunted.

All the cars apart from Franco promised Race Control that they would not overtake on the dangerous corner.

‘Go race!’ ordered Race Control.

'GO, FRANCO! GO, MARCO!' chanted the fans.

The whistles blew for Franco.

The banners and flags flew for Franco.

The crowd screamed for Franco to go fast.

But the only thing Franco saw was Marco, his younger team-mate, in front of him on the grid for his favourite race.

Franco saw red!

1,2,3,4,5 lights out!

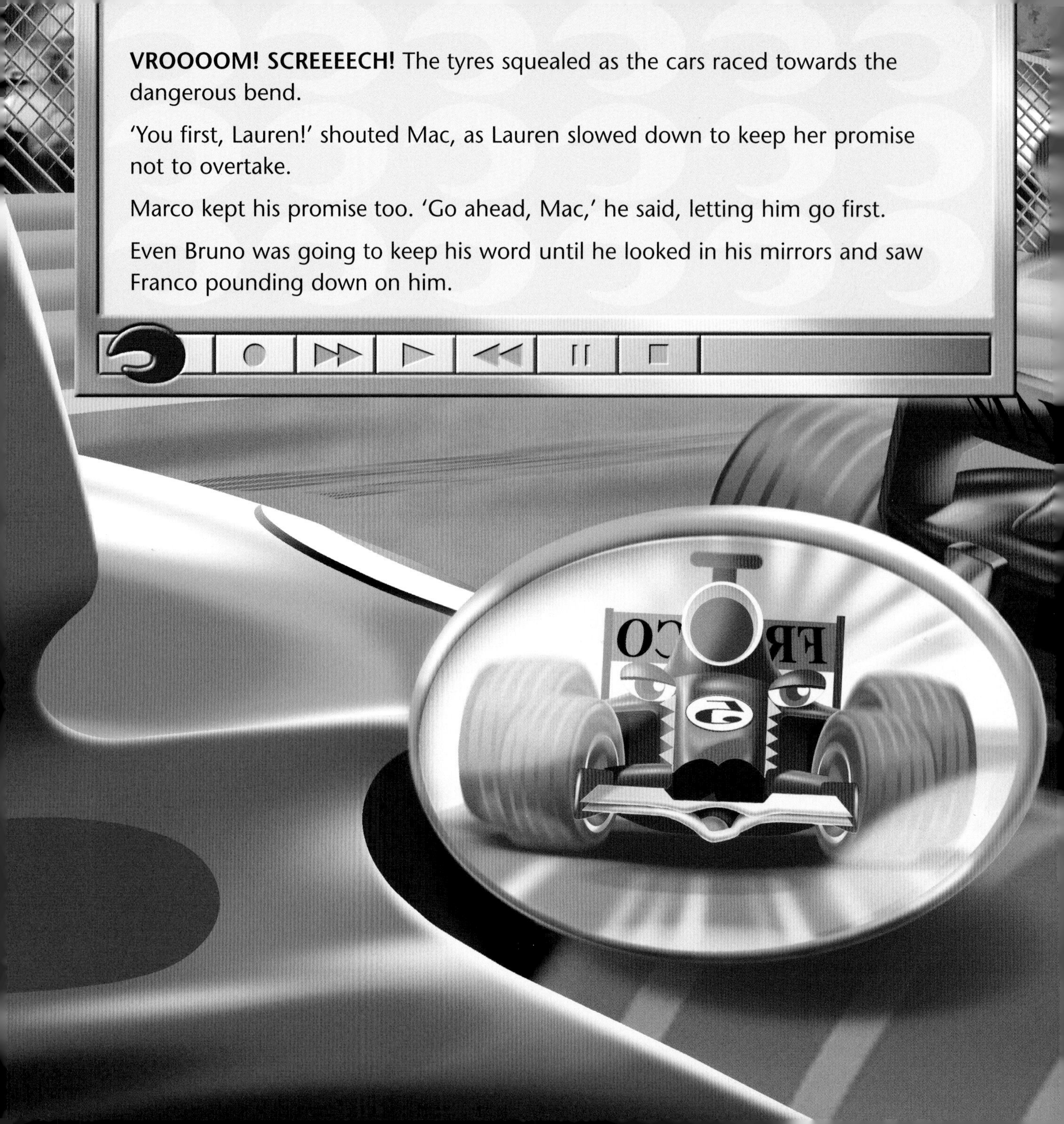

VROOOOM! SCREEEECH! The tyres squealed as the cars raced towards the dangerous bend.

'You first, Lauren!' shouted Mac, as Lauren slowed down to keep her promise not to overtake.

Marco kept his promise too. 'Go ahead, Mac,' he said, letting him go first.

Even Bruno was going to keep his word until he looked in his mirrors and saw Franco pounding down on him.

6
6
CO
MAC
1
AC
LAUREN
POSITION
1st
2nd
3rd
4th
5th

WHOOSH! Bruno never touched the brakes as he zoomed past Marco.

'Bravo! Bravo!' The crowd cheered Bruno's bravery.

'I'm glad they don't know about the promise,' thought Bruno.

BRUNO

5
5
FRANCO

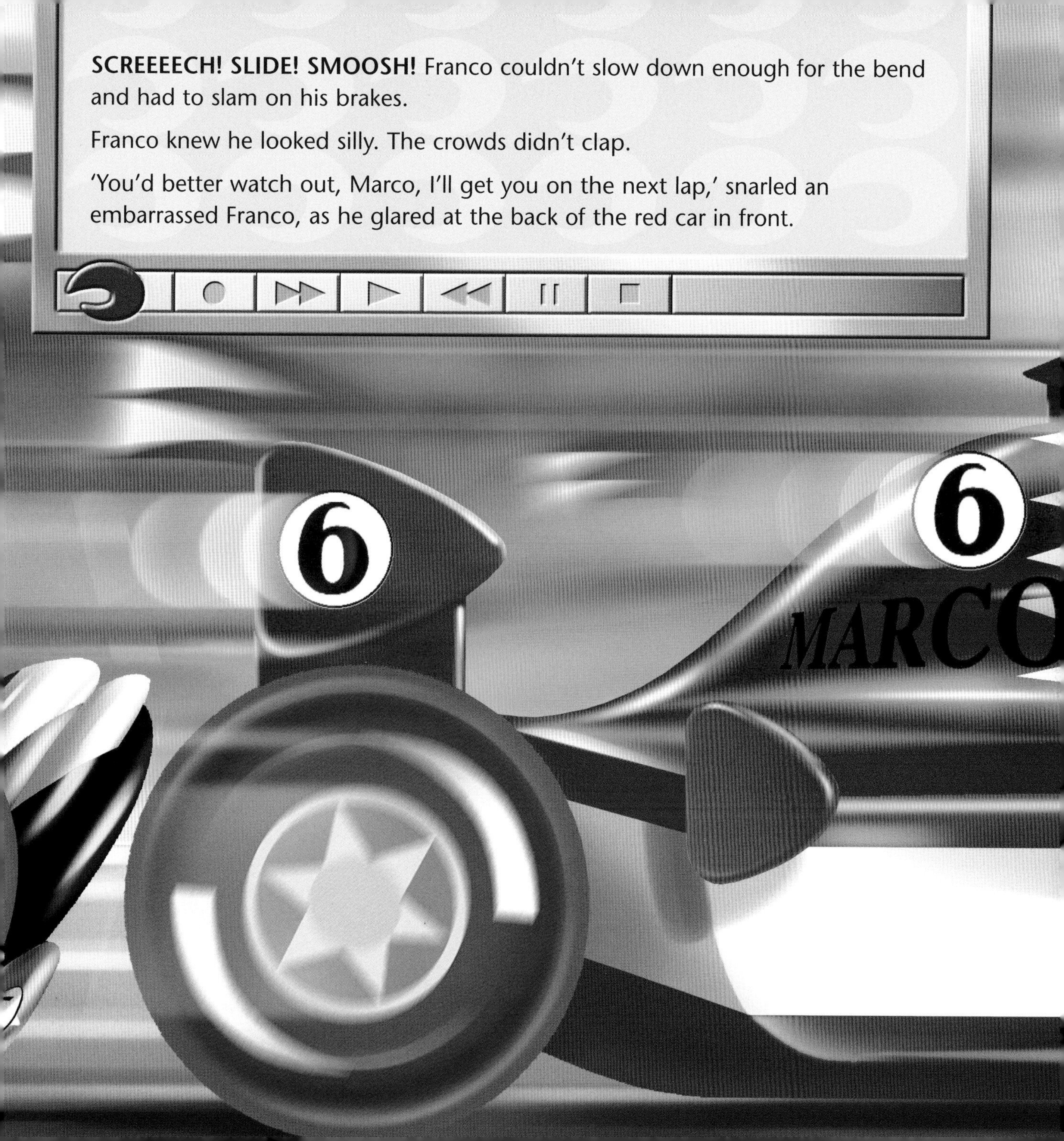

SCREEEECH! SLIDE! SMOOSH! Franco couldn't slow down enough for the bend and had to slam on his brakes.

Franco knew he looked silly. The crowds didn't clap.

'You'd better watch out, Marco, I'll get you on the next lap,' snarled an embarrassed Franco, as he glared at the back of the red car in front.

Bruno liked the attention. He thundered down the straight at top speed and the crowd jumped up, clapping and stomping its feet for him. As he smiled up at the grandstands, he forgot about the bumpy chicane.

Bump! Bang! Wallop! Bruno bounced from one bump to the next before landing in the middle of the track.

BRUNO
3
3

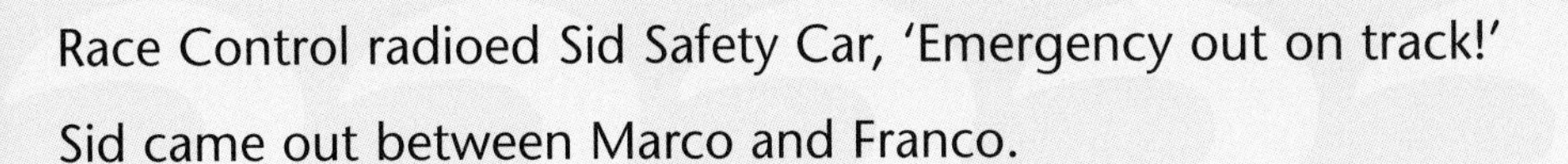

Race Control radioed Sid Safety Car, 'Emergency out on track!'

Sid came out between Marco and Franco.

As Lauren came round the track she saw Franco up ahead and remembered how mean he had been to Marco.

'You haven't been a good sport today, so it is your own fault that Marco is beating you!' she said.

'We'll see about that,' screeched Franco, as he zoomed past a startled Sid.

SID

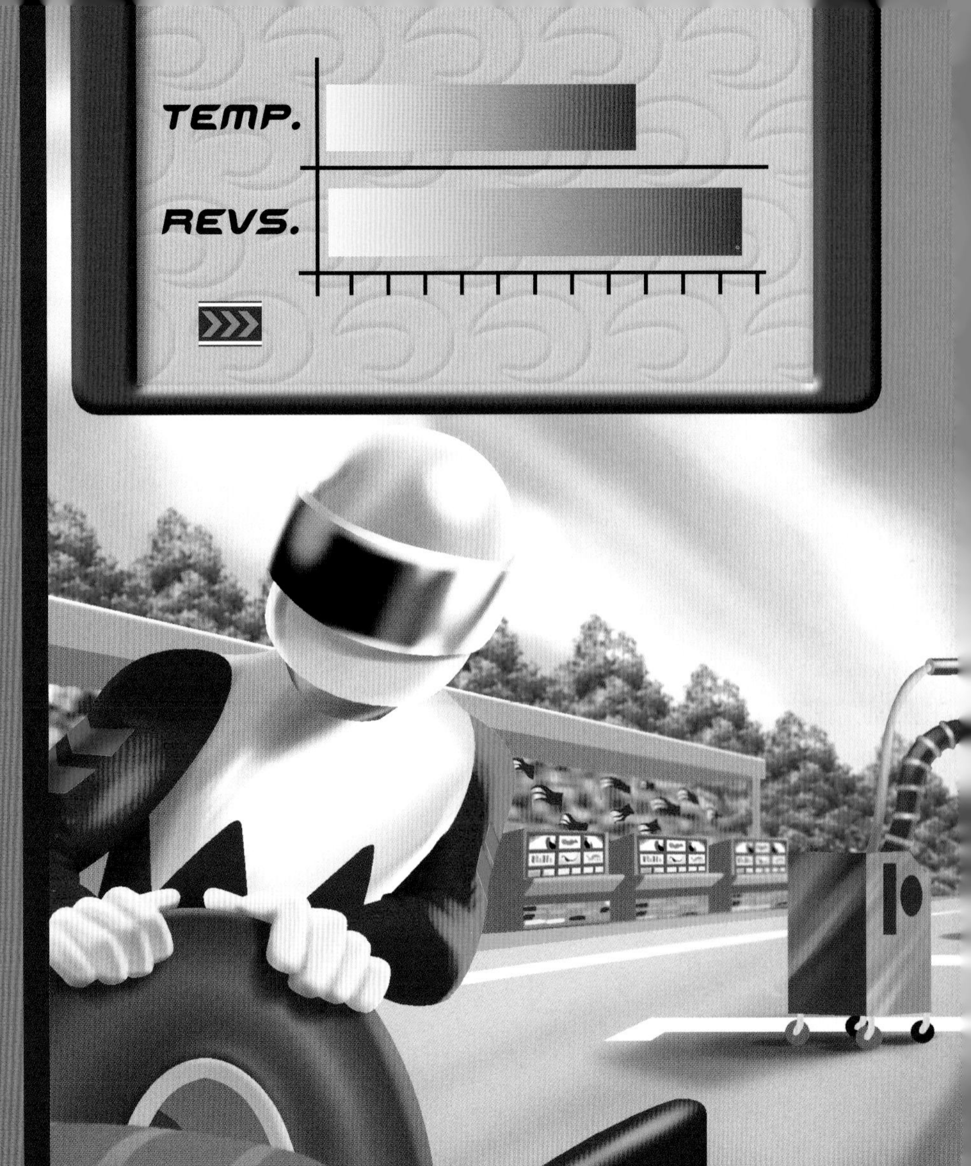
TEMP.
REVS.

'Oh, no!' shouted the crowd sadly as Race Control signalled Franco.

'No overtaking the safety car! Your penalty is to stop for ten seconds in the pits!' ordered an angry Race Control.

Franco was really seeing red. His engine screamed in a temper while he waited for the lollipop to go up and let him back on the track.

empty
FUEL
full

Vroom! Vroom! went Franco's engine, as he re-joined the track behind Maddy and Roxy. Furious to be behind the girls, he drove faster and faster not watching his fuel.

'Come in next lap for fuel, Marco,' warned Pit Board.

6
6
BRAKE
1
MAC
1

'Faster, Marco! Win the race!' shouted the crowd.

'I'll show him who is boss,' he thought, as he swerved in front of Marco in the pit entrance and took his place for the pit stop.

Poor Marco was losing time as he waited for the team to get everything ready.

Mac could see how upset Marco was as he waited for his fuel. 'The only way you can beat Marco is by playing tricks, Franco,' scolded Mac.

'I'm the star in the team and I'll do what I like!' retorted Franco.

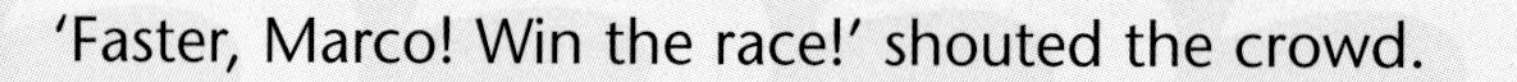

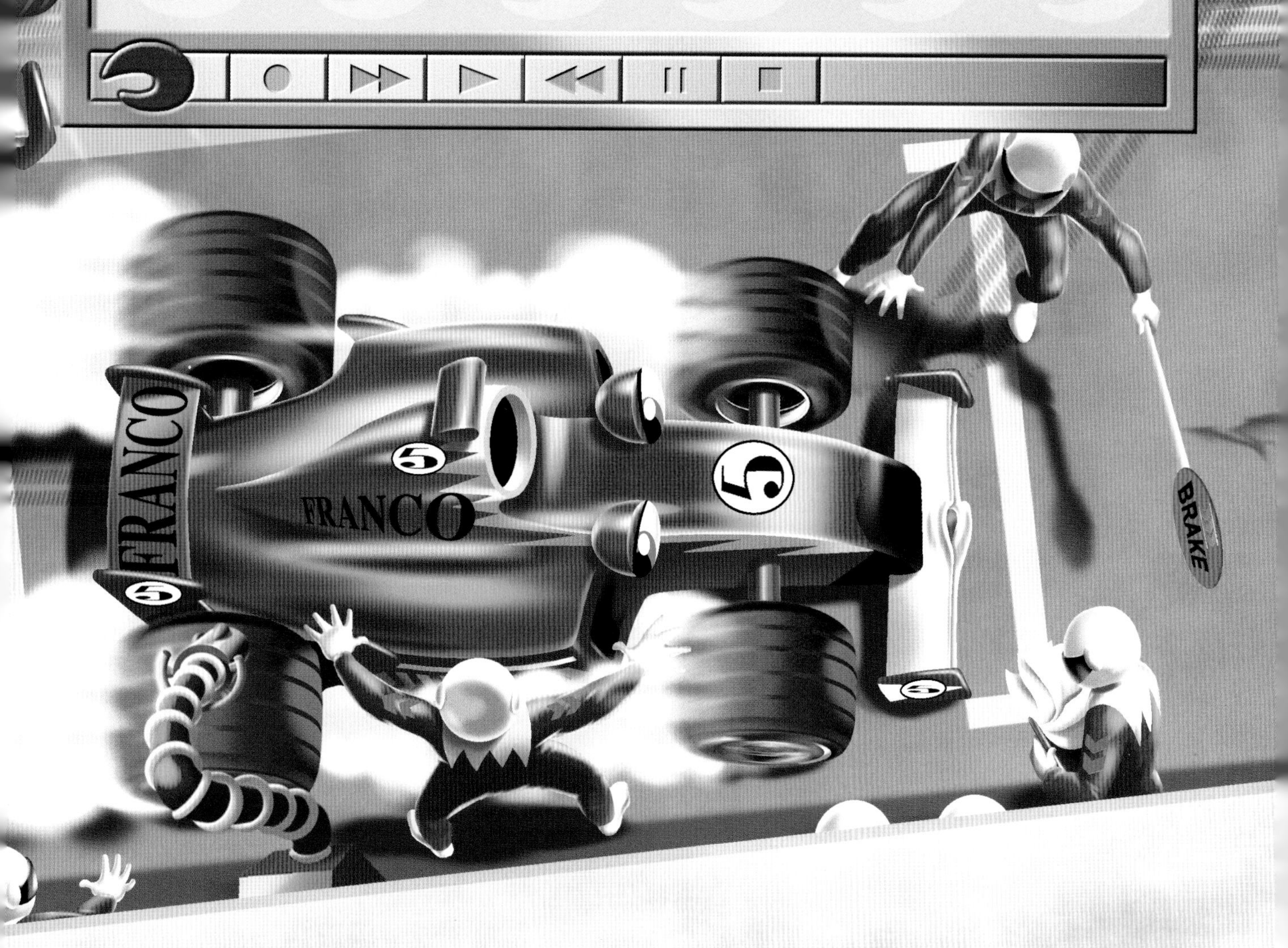

BRAKE
5

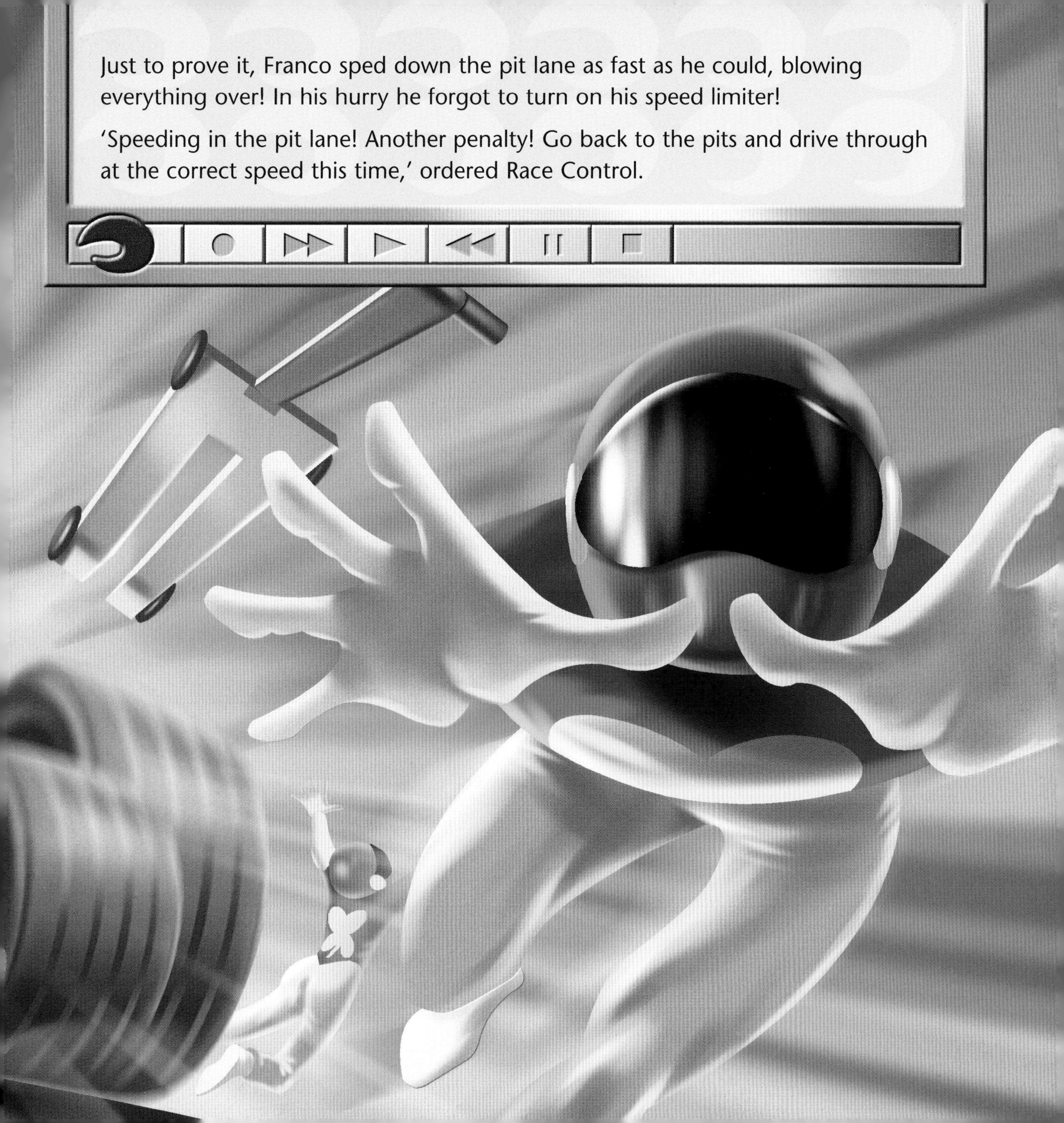

Just to prove it, Franco sped down the pit lane as fast as he could, blowing everything over! In his hurry he forgot to turn on his speed limiter!

'Speeding in the pit lane! Another penalty! Go back to the pits and drive through at the correct speed this time,' ordered Race Control.

Franco could feel all the fans pointing and staring as he drove round to the pits for his penalty. He was ashamed and very miserable to have his fans so cross with him.

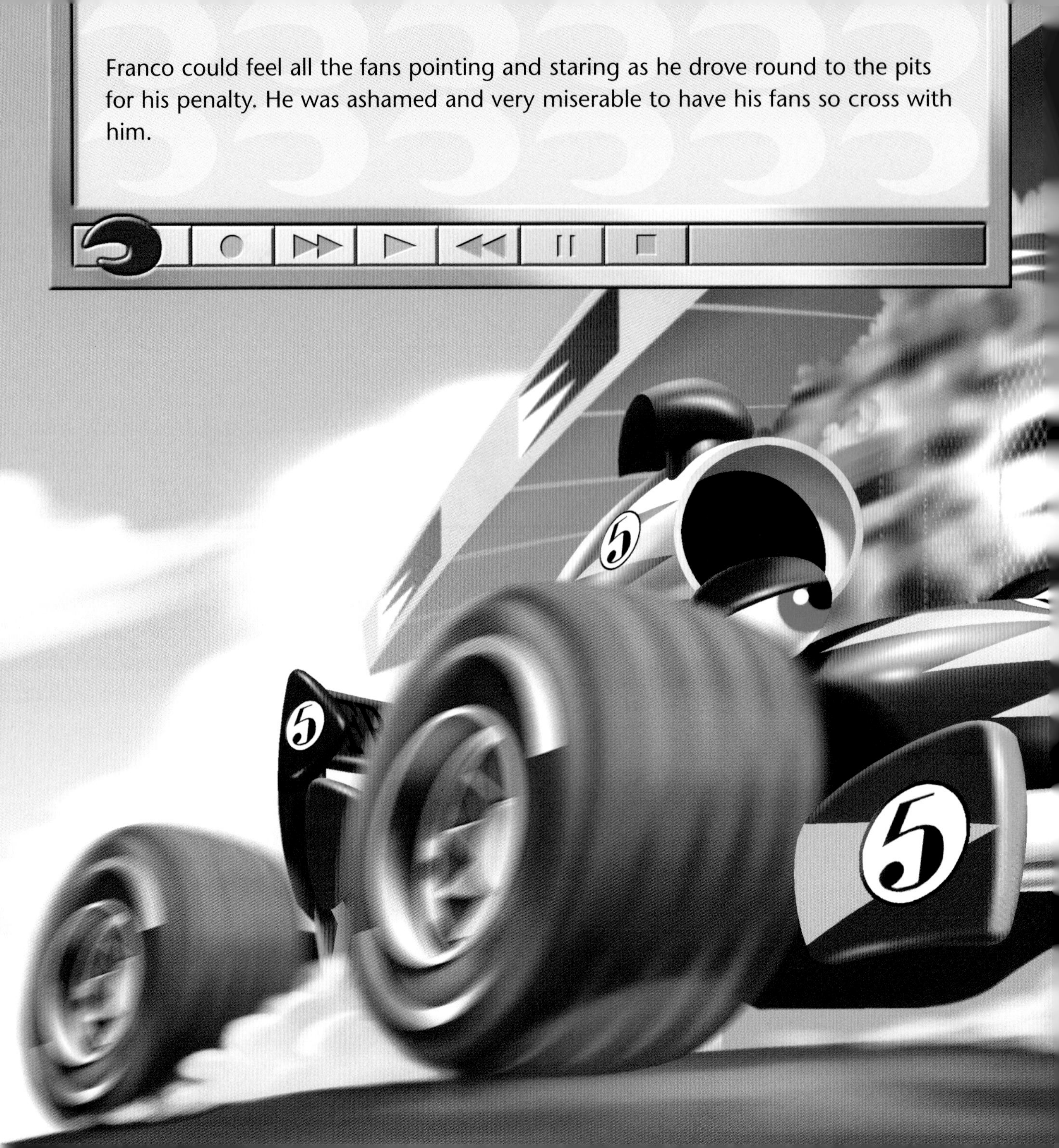

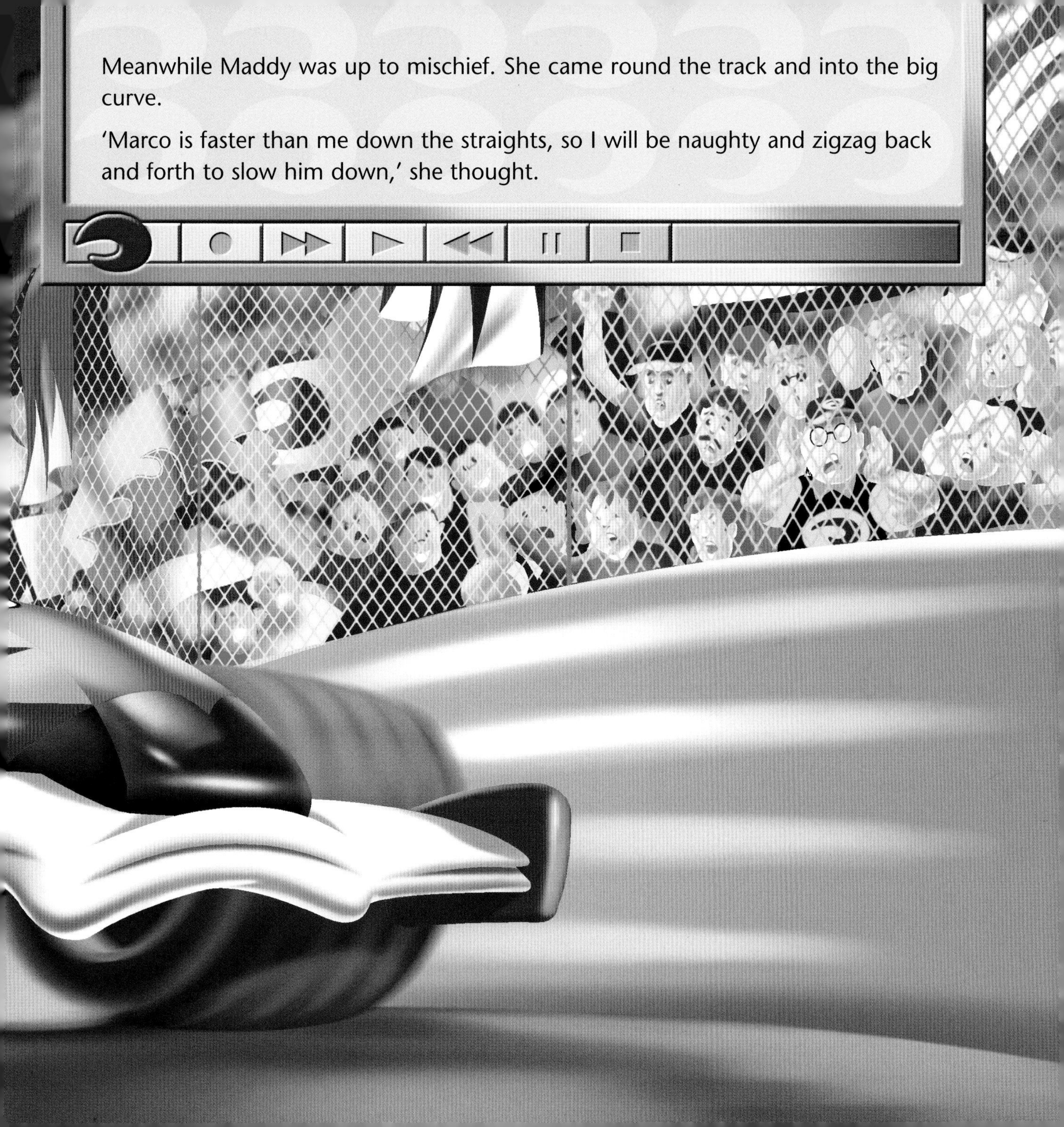

Meanwhile Maddy was up to mischief. She came round the track and into the big curve.

'Marco is faster than me down the straights, so I will be naughty and zigzag back and forth to slow him down,' she thought.

MADDY
MADDY

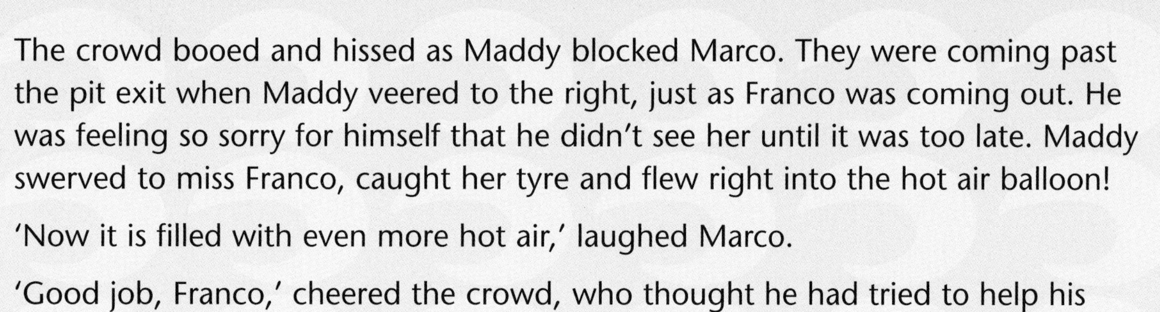

The crowd booed and hissed as Maddy blocked Marco. They were coming past the pit exit when Maddy veered to the right, just as Franco was coming out. He was feeling so sorry for himself that he didn't see her until it was too late. Maddy swerved to miss Franco, caught her tyre and flew right into the hot air balloon!

'Now it is filled with even more hot air,' laughed Marco.

'Good job, Franco,' cheered the crowd, who thought he had tried to help his team-mate.

'I can't win the race, but I can win my fans back by helping Marco,' thought Franco.

Franco was just wondering how he could help, when he looked up on the giant scoreboard and saw Marco was in first place, with Mac and Lauren close behind. On the screen he could see that Marco was in trouble. One brake was so hot it was on fire.

Franco hatched a brave plan. He slowed down and on the last lap he set off his fire extinguisher just as Marco went past and cooled down his brake. Marco crossed the finish line and the crowd went wild.

'We love Marco! We love Franco!' roared the adoring fans. Franco had saved the day and was the crowd's hero!

For once, Franco was happy to share the spotlight with Marco.
'Thanks, Mac and Lauren. You were right about teamwork. I didn't win the race and I look awful, but my fans still love me!' Franco said with a smile.

RACE INFORMATION

CAR GRAPHICS

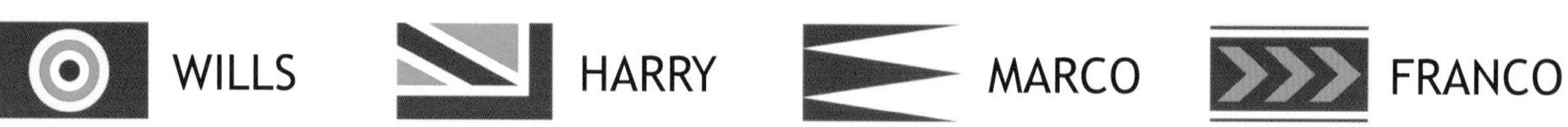

 MAC

 LAUREN

ROXY

 LUCKY

 WILLS

 HARRY

MARCO

 FRANCO

 MADDY

BRUNO

INFORMATION SCREENS

SPEED
— shows lap times

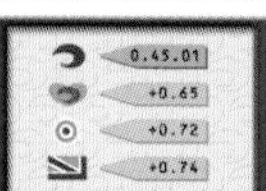

RACE POSITION
— shows leader

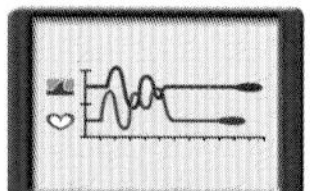
TELEMETRY
— shows technical info

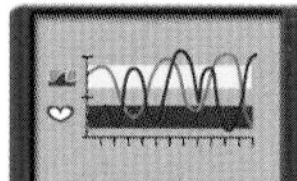
TEMPERATURE
— temperature read-out

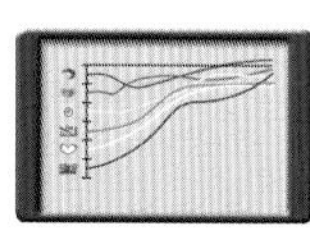
REVS
— shows engine rpm

FLAG
— shows current situation
on track

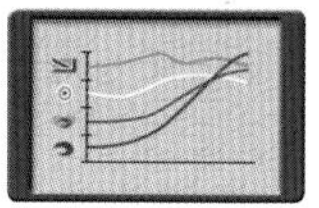
ACCELERATION
— shows acceleration